AF654222

THINKO

Om KIDZ
An imprint of Om Books International

Om Kidz | Om Books International

Reprinted in 2024

Corporate & Editorial Office
A-12, Sector 64, Noida 201 301
Uttar Pradesh, India
Phone: +91 120 477 4100
Email: editorial@ombooks.com
Website: www.ombooksinternational.com

ISBN: 978-93-84625-11-5

Printed in India

10 9 8 7 6

Sales Office
107, Ansari Road, Darya Ganj
New Delhi 110 002, India
Phone: +91 11 4000 9000
Email: sales@ombooks.com
Website: www.ombooks.com

THINKO

I'm all set to read

Paste your photograph here

My name is

Rob was always in trouble. Whether it was a fist fight with the neighbourhood kids or his lunch getting stolen from school or someone calling him names, he just didn't know how to save himself.

Rob was very obedient in school and at home. His teachers and parents were proud of him. But not being able to handle bullies really upset him.

He'd hide in his room on many days. On some days, he would just stay in bed, feeling sad and helpless. Rob needed help.

"I don't want to go to school today," Rob told his mother one day.

"Why not, Rob?" asked his mother.

"Everybody teases me. They snatch my books. They tear my homework. I can't go," Rob cried bitterly. But he had no choice. He had to go to school.

That day, Rob sat at a corner desk in his classroom.

"Hey, Rob! You're here. We've been looking for you all over," shouted one of his classmates.

Rob pretended to hide behind a book. He knew what was coming.

But there was no hiding from the bullies.

They snatched the book from Rob and tore it page by page. Rob could not even meet their eyes.

Rob waited for the bullies to leave, trying very hard not to cry.

The bullies put the torn pages in his hands and laughed as they left.

Before going to bed that night, Rob prayed hard for a bully-free life. Just then, there was a flash of light in his room. Rob opened his eyes to see what it was.

Slowly, the light faded and he saw something red and round. He reached out to get it.

THINKO

It was a red hat! It had “Thinko” written on it.

Under the hat was a note, “Hello, Thinko! Welcome to the Superhero Club. When you wear this hat, you will become Thinko, the quick-thinking superhero! This hat will help you think of quick ways to get out of trouble.”

Rob could not believe what just happened. He held the hat in his hand and fell asleep.

The next morning, he got ready to go to school before his mother could wake him up. He kept the hat safely in his bag before he left.

When he reached his class, he went to sit in the corner. But he remembered the hat, so he turned around and sat in the first row.

Soon, the bullies entered and walked towards him. He looked at them and got up. But he wasn't running away. He wore the red hat. He was Thinko!

One of the bullies pushed him aside, sat in his place and picked up his book. Just when he tore the first page, Rob shouted, "Look, teacher. He's tearing my book. He tears it everyday!"

"Is this true?" the teacher asked the bully. "Er...no...I..." the bully didn't know what to say.

THINKO

The teacher took the bully out of the class and called his parents.

Rob was happy. They would not trouble him anymore. He took off his hat and put it carefully into his bag.

THIN

The hat helped Rob get out of trouble. He went home and told his mother what happened, leaving out the part where he was Thinko the Superhero.

Rob's mother heard him and felt very proud. She was happy that Rob had come back smiling from school after a very long time!

That night, Rob hugged the hat and went to sleep.

When he woke up, the hat was gone!

"Mother, did you see my red hat? I can't find it anywhere!" Rob came yelling out of his room.

"What red hat?" asked his mother.

Rob had not told his mother about the red hat and how he had become Thinko the Superhero.

"Oh! Nothing! Never mind," replied Rob as he went back to his room. Rob's mother smiled.

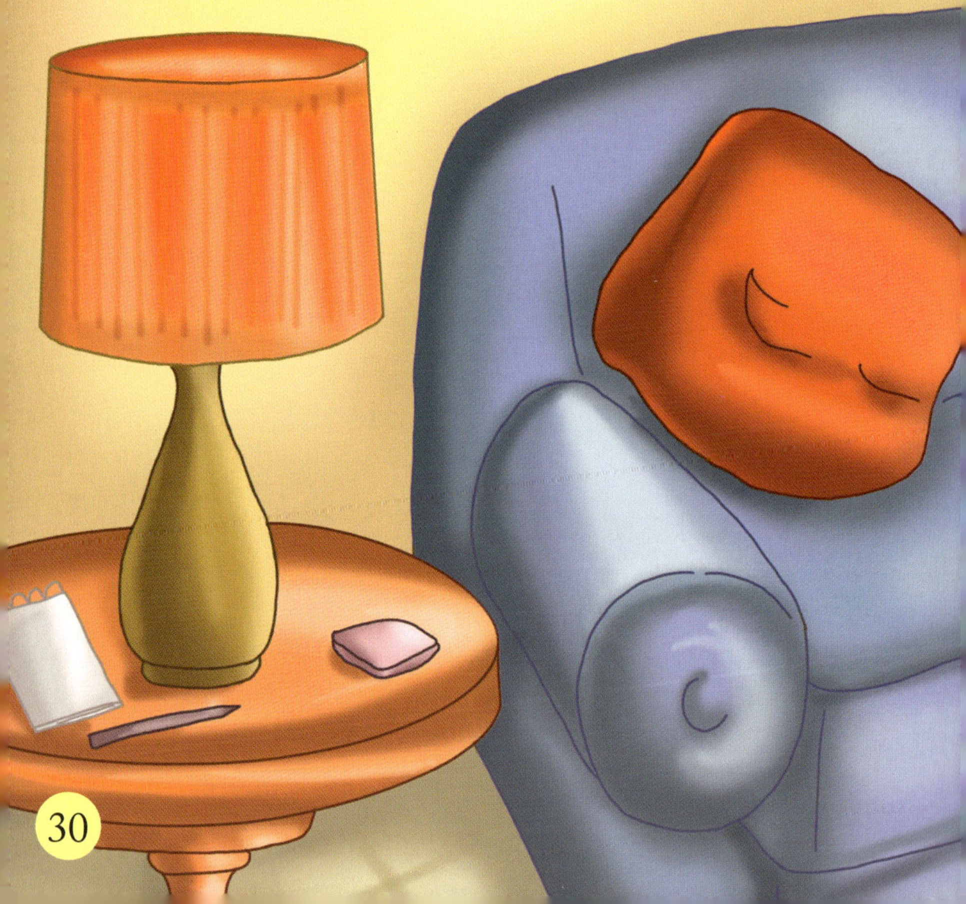

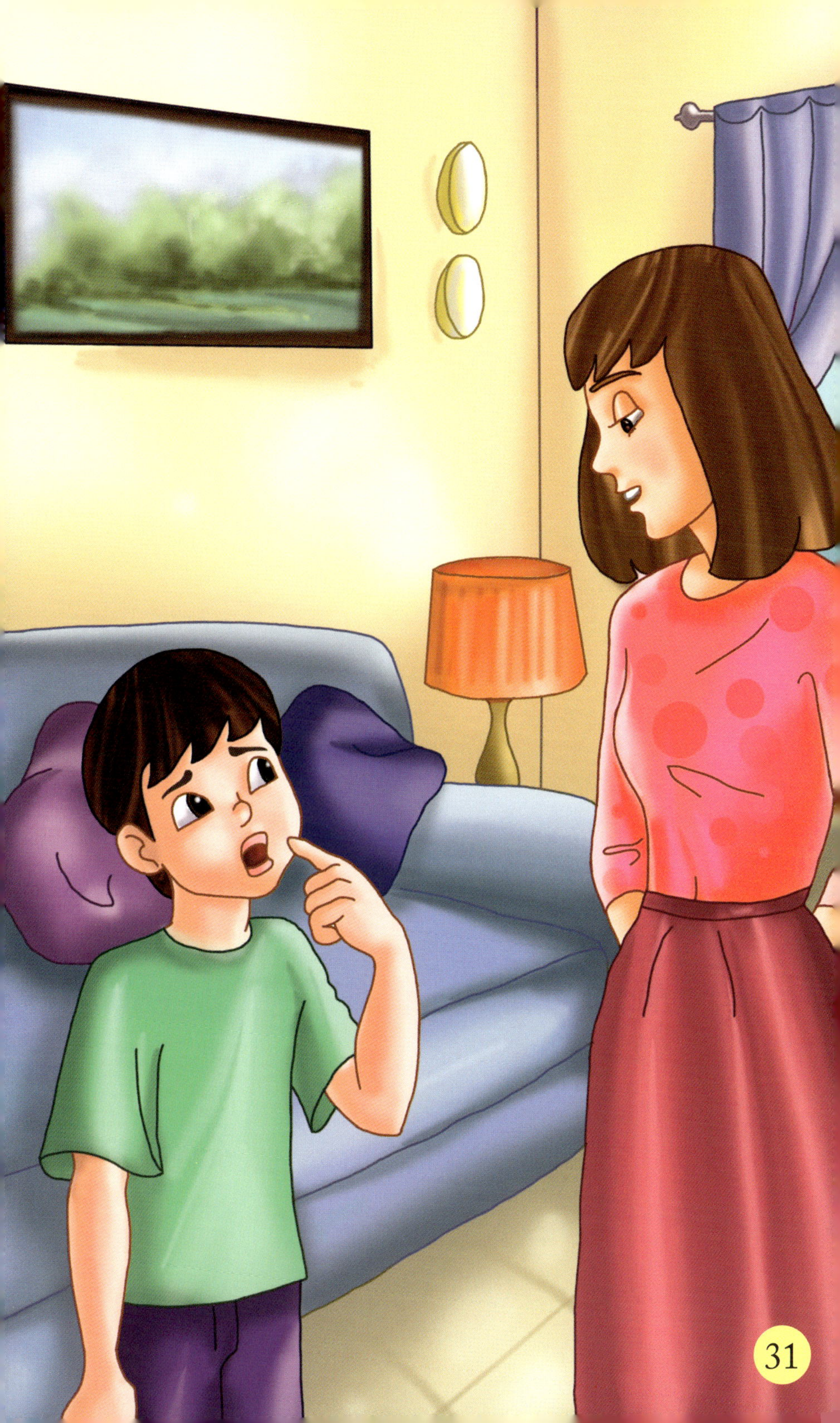

No bully ever came close to Rob in school since that day. In fact, they became friends.

Rob's mother had put the red hat back in her closet. It was her idea all along! All she did was help Rob think like a superhero.